HOW I WENT SHOPPING AND WHAT I GOT

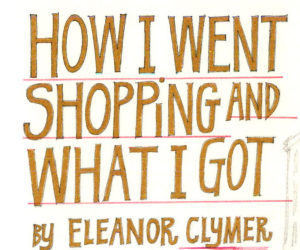

HOW I WENT SHOPPING AND WHAT I GOT

BY ELEANOR CLYMER

ILLUSTRATED BY
TRINA SCHART HYMAN

HOLT, RINEHART AND WINSTON, INC.
NEW YORK • CHICAGO • SAN FRANCISCO

OTHER BOOKS BY ELEANOR CLYMER

THE BIG PILE OF DIRT

MY BROTHER STEVIE

THE SECOND GREATEST INVENTION

SEARCH FOR A LIVING FOSSIL

WHEELS

1685642

This is about something that happened to me last spring.

My name is Debra Brown and I'm thirteen. I was twelve when it happened.

I have a father and mother. My father works in the Post Office. I have a brother Dave, sixteen, and a little sister and brother, Judy and Benny. They're six and seven. I'm sort of in the middle.

My brother Dave is very smart. He gets all A's and is talented in music. The school let him borrow a clarinet that's worth $200. Now my parents are getting him one, and he's working to help pay for it. He wants to play in a symphony orchestra.

My little brother Benny is very good but he's sick a lot. He's allergic.

My little sister Judy is very smart and cute, but she's spoiled. She always gets her way, especially with my father. And she's always into everything.

Then there's me. I'm just normal. I go to school and do my homework and help around the house. I baby-sit and go to the store and wash the dishes—things like that. I get the paper for my father, and I listen to Dave play his clarinet and tell him how it sounds, if he asks me. A clarinet is okay, but I always thought it would be nice to play a trumpet. I heard a trumpet player give a concert in school once and I just loved the way it sounded—sort of faraway and mysterious.

1

Well, I always took it for granted that I would do the things I do, and I was glad when my mother said I was a big help. I liked it when my teacher praised me in school. I was so good it was sickening.

Then things changed. I met these two girls, Joanne and Marcy. They were about a year older than me. We started doing things together. We'd go to the movies, or go to Joanne's house and try on her mother's eyelashes, or just fool around. They loved to hang around music stores listening to records and meeting boys.

I didn't like the records much. I like music, but not rock all the time. Also I wasn't so good at talking and kidding with boys as they were. Still it was fun.

We stayed out late. We slept over at Joanne's house and talked all night. It was exciting. They didn't care if they never studied. So I didn't like to show that I did, because I wanted them to like me. More and more I got thinking the way they did.

When I said I had to go home, Joanne said, Oh, what for? You'll just have to work.

So I thought, She's right. They just want me home to work. Why doesn't Dave help? All he does is practice. I'd like to practice too but I know Mama would never buy me a trumpet. What's the use of asking?

So I didn't ask. I wanted things and got mad but I didn't say anything.

Mama saw something was wrong but she just said, Debbie, I don't know why you're sulking like that. Now cheer up and be a good girl.

That made me even madder.

Well, one time Joanne and Marcy were going to go shopping on Saturday. Joanne just loves to shop. Her mother gives her money and lets her buy all her clothes. She'll buy stuff one week and take it back the next. They asked me to go and I said I would. Joanne wanted to get shoes. Marcy wanted a skirt and sweater. They asked me what I wanted to get and I said, Oh, maybe I'll see some-thing nice. I was sort of hoping I'd find some marvelous thing but I didn't know what.

I didn't tell Mama we were going because I thought she would say I couldn't. I thought I'd wait till Saturday and then just go out.

But Saturday morning my mother said, Debbie, you will have to mind Judy because I have to take Benny to the clinic. He's been coughing.

I said, Oh, Mama, I was going out with Joanne and Marcy. We were going shopping.

She said, Debbie, you didn't tell me. Besides, you have no money for shopping and you don't need any-thing.

That made me mad, even though I knew it was true. I only had my allowance, and that was for lunch and car-fare, and about four dollars I saved from baby-sitting.

I said, Well, I told them I would go. Can't you take Judy with you?

She said, No, Debbie, you know how restless Judy is. Now you play with her and let her watch TV and I'll get back as soon as I can.

So she left with Benny and there I was stuck with Judy. I kept thinking, It isn't fair. Why can't Dave baby-sit sometimes?

Judy wanted me to play with her but I wouldn't. I

told her to leave me alone. So she went in the bathroom and played with water, and got all wet. I had to mop the floor and put dry clothes on her.

Then the doorbell rang and there were Joanne and Marcy saying, Are you ready?

I said, No, I have to baby-sit.

Marcy looked disappointed and said, Oh, that's too bad. I wanted you to help me pick out a skirt and sweater.

But Joanne just said, Well, good-by, we'll see you later.

And they were just going when Judy started to yell, I want to go, I want to go.

I told her, Be quiet, you can't go.

Then Joanne said, Hey, why not?

I asked, Why not what?

She said, Take her along.

I said, That's a crazy idea. My mother would have a fit.

But Joanne liked the idea. She said, No, it isn't crazy, we can watch her, and then you can go. We'll tell your mother we made you do it. We'll say Judy yelled and we had to take her.

I knew that wasn't right. By that time I didn't want to go at all, but they stood there looking at me and saying, Oh, come on! So I said okay.

I told Judy, You can come but you have to be good. If you're not good I'll leave you there.

She looked scared and said, I'll be good.

I put her new red coat and hat on her, and put on my best sweater, and we started. Judy hung on to Joanne's hand and jumped up and down, she was so excited at going with the big girls.

Joanne bought her some gum in the subway and she sat there chewing and swinging her feet, and people looked at her and smiled. She did look cute. She's a real pretty kid.

When we got to the store there was a big crowd because they were having sales. Judy didn't want to hold my hand.

I said, You stay with me. If you get lost in this crowd I'll never find you.

So she hung on to me with all her might, and I said, You don't need to hold so tight. So she let go of me and took Joanne's hand.

There was a sale of sweaters. There were about a million of them piled on tables, and we began helping Marcy find some. Joanne found a real hot one, pink and purple. I found one with fringes. When we had about six, Marcy wanted to go to the dressing room to try them on. We started to go there and suddenly I said, Where's Judy? Joanne, wasn't she with you?

Joanne said, Yes, she was, but I don't see her now.

I called, Judy, where are you?

Then I saw her way off looking at some stuffed

animals on a table. Just then she pulled one and a whole pile fell on the floor. I ran over to pick them up and said, Judy, remember what I said. You must be good.

She said, I didn't mean to do it.

We went to help Marcy try on the sweaters. Trying on clothes is fun. We all squeezed into the dressing room with about a hundred other people. There were some pretty funny-looking ladies in there, especially in their underwear. We giggled at them and teased Marcy about how she looked in the sweaters till she said, I don't want any of them. Let's go look at shoes.

So we went to the shoe department in the basement. The shoes were all mixed up on tables. You had to find your right size and try on one shoe at a time because they were tied together in pairs. I found a pair of sandals and was hopping around on one foot, and some lady bumped into me and nearly knocked me over.

Joanne wanted to try on some high-heeled boots. I held her pocketbook and she sat down on the floor and pulled one on and then she couldn't get up and we almost got hysterical.

Suddenly I missed Judy again. I yelled, Judy, where are you? And I heard her yell back, I'm over here. I can't see you!

Poor kid, she was sort of buried among all those ladies. I could remember how it felt to be little, down there among big people's legs, but I wouldn't let myself be sorry for her. I told her to lean against a counter and we'd be through soon.

Joanne got the boot off and said, I'll take these.

My mother will have a fit but I can bring them back next week.

Just then Judy called out, I have to go to the bathroom.

Can't you wait? I asked her. But she said no.

So I said, Joanne, you and Marcy wait here for us. And we went up on the escalator. As soon as we got on that, Judy was perfectly happy. She didn't want to get off. When we got to the ladies' room, she didn't need to go.

I told her, Well, we're here now, so you go. So she did, and when we got back on the escalator she didn't want to get off.

Then Marcy wanted to find a skirt or some pants, but Judy complained, I'm hungry.

I said, We'll have lunch later. But she insisted, I'm hungry now. Let's go home.

I told the girls, I better take her home. And I thought to myself, What did I come for anyhow?

But Joanne had an idea. There's a snack bar here. We'll go and get her some lunch. Then we can shop some more. Maybe you'll find something.

At the snack bar Judy asked for a hot dog. She took a bite of it and said, I don't like it.

I said, Judy, you said you were hungry. Now eat it.

So she put relish on it but then she wouldn't eat it,

and asked for ice cream. I got her some ice cream and the rest of us had Cokes. I wasn't hungry at all. We paid and went to look for Marcy's skirt. On the way we passed the toy department, and Judy pulled my hand and said, Debbie, look! Dolls!

I said, We can't stop. We must find Marcy a skirt.

But she pulled back and pulled back till I got mad and said, All right. If you want to stay here, you stay. I'll come back for you later.

And I left her in front of the doll counter and ran after the girls.

Joanne asked, Where's Judy?

I said, She's looking at some dolls. I told her to stay there and I'd come back for her.

Joanne said, Oh? Well, maybe we should find something for you while she's there. What do you want to get?

I couldn't think of anything in that whole store that I wanted. I really wanted just to go home. But I didn't say so. We started looking for Marcy's skirt.

But I began to feel awful. I thought, It was mean to leave a little kid like that alone. Then I told myself that she wanted to come and she promised to be good.

I felt as if there were two people inside, arguing.

I heard Marcy saying, Hey Debbie, I'm talking to you. How do you like this skirt?

I said, Wait here. I'm going to get Judy.

I ran to the escalator and pushed past all the people on it and got to the doll counter.

Judy wasn't there.

I called, Judy, where are you?

No answer.

I thought, That kid never does what I tell her. She's going to get it when I find her.

I looked all around the doll department.

Then I thought, Maybe she's looking at bikes. She's been asking for a bike. But she wasn't near the

bikes. I looked all over. There were a billion shelves full of games, piled up almost to the ceiling. You could hardly see a little kid in all that stuff. I called, Judy, you come out here now or you'll be sorry.

But there was no answer. I began to get scared.

I asked the lady at the doll counter, Did you see a little girl in a red coat and hat?

She said, Yes, but that was quite a while ago.

I asked, Where did she go? She said, I really didn't notice. She was standing here, and then she went away.

Then I thought, Maybe she went to look for us. But she wouldn't know where to find us.

I ran back down the escalator to Marcy and Joanne.

16

I said, I can't find her. She isn't there.

Joanne said, You're kidding.

I said, No. She was there but she went away.

Joanne said, We'll go back and look. She must be hiding up there. So we went back and looked over that entire floor, but no Judy.

Then I was so scared I almost couldn't breathe. I was shaking. What could have happened? I thought, Did somebody kidnap her?

I said, What'll I do?

The lady at the counter said, You better go to the office. They'll help you. Don't worry. People lose kids here every day. We always find them.

We went to the top floor and told the manager that we had lost a little girl. He asked her name and what she looked like, and then he spoke over the loud-speaker.

Attention shoppers. A little girl has been lost. Her name is Judy Brown and she has black eyes and curly hair and is wearing a red coat and hat. If you see her, please bring her to the office on the top floor.

He repeated it three times. Meanwhile we sat on a bench and waited. I felt cold. I put my hands in my sweater sleeves and shivered.

We waited and nothing happened. The man said to us, We will repeat the message in a few minutes. Meantime we just have to wait.

But I couldn't just sit there. I had to do something. I tried to think what Judy would do. She might be hiding because she was afraid I would yell at her. She sometimes did that at home. I told the man, I will go and start looking for her, and if somebody brings her here you keep her.

He thought that was a good idea. I said we should separate and all go to different places and then come back.

Marcy said, She's so little, how would we see her?

I told her, She has on a red coat and hat. You'll see her.

Joanne said, Okay, come on. We better hurry, we have to go home soon.

Then I started looking. I went to the ladies' room and asked the matron. I looked in the phone booths. I went to every place we had been. No Judy. So I went back to the office.

Joanne and Marcy were there already. The manager came over and said he would make another announcement, but still nothing happened.

Marcy said, You know what? I'm hungry. We didn't really eat any lunch and it's three o'clock.

I looked at the clock. I couldn't believe it. I thought my mother must be home by now, wondering where we were.

I knew I would have to phone her. I began to shiver again, trying to think what I'd tell her.

Then the manager came over and said, Girls, we can't do any more. We've had the store detective looking, and I don't think she's in the store. We'll have to call the police.

I said, Oh, no!

He said, Well, first you'd better call your mother.

Joanne and Marcy were looking at me as if they were thinking there wasn't anything more we could do. All of a sudden I couldn't stand the sight of them.

I told them, Look, you two go on home. It's no

use your sitting here. I'll wait a while, then I'll look some more.

Joanne said, You think we should?

I said, Yes, go on home. I'll call my mother from a phone booth.

The manager said, You can use this phone.

But I didn't want anybody to hear me. I started for the ladies' room. Joanne and Marcy started to come with me. I said to them, Don't come, I'll go in here and phone, and I'll see you later.

Joanne said, Okay. Gee, it's too bad. And you didn't even get anything!

And they left.

I went to a phone booth and dialed and thought, I hope Mama's not home.

But she picked up the phone at the first ring.

I said, Mama, this is Debbie.

She asked, Debbie, where are you?

I said, I did something terrible.

She gasped out, What happened?

I said, Joanne and Marcy and I, we went shopping and took Judy along.

She told me, Well, you shouldn't have, but why didn't you leave me a note? Did you eat something?

I said, Yes, but the thing is, you know Judy, she started playing tricks and now I can't find her.

She screamed at me, You can't *find* her! What do you mean?

I could hardly talk. I said, I looked everywhere. The manager of the store put it on the loudspeaker and they didn't find her, but I'm going to look some more.

Mama said, Let me talk to the manager.

I said, I can't, I'm in a booth. I have to go now. She must be in the store. Don't worry. Good-by.

She yelled at me, Debbie! Wait! What store? Where are you?

I said, I can't wait. I have to find her. Don't worry, I won't come home without her.

And I hung up.

I must have been crazy to leave my mother there, not knowing where I was or anything. But I was so upset I didn't know what I was doing.

I started looking. I was on the top floor and I walked through that whole store. I walked around each floor and went down on the escalator because I knew Judy liked it and might be riding on it. But I didn't find her. Finally I got down to the street floor. I looked at all those people pawing through piles of things under the bright lights, and I hated them. I hated myself too.

Then I went out on the street. The street lamps were lit, and the lights in the tall buildings. I looked way, way up, and in the little piece of sky between the

1685642

buildings a plane was going past with its red and green lights blinking.

I thought, It would be nice to be up there, flying away somewhere. I would have liked to fly away from myself. Only I had to go home. I had to walk in the door and say, I lost my sister.

They would look at me and say, You lost Judy? You get out. We don't want you here any more.

I wouldn't blame them. It wasn't just an accident. A part of me wanted to lose her.

I thought, Maybe I better not go home at all. I could run away. Go to Detroit. I have an aunt there. But I only had four dollars. I couldn't go to Detroit with four dollars.

Well, there was nothing else for me to do so I went down in the subway. It was crowded. Everybody was going home, with lots of bundles and tired kids, laughing and talking and eating candy. They all seemed so happy. I was the only one that wasn't. I felt as if I was all alone in the whole world. The train rocked and rattled, and at every station people got off. I sat down, I was so tired.

At last the train got to my station. It was dark outside. I walked to our house, up the stairs and in the door.

There was a scream.

Debbie! Debbie's home!

And there was Judy. She was jumping up and down, yelling. She threw herself at me and hugged me. Then Mama started talking and hugging me, and so did Dave and Benny, till I thought I would fall on the floor. And all of them screaming, Where were you? Why didn't you call us? What's the matter with you?

Finally Mama said, Leave her alone a minute, let her catch her breath.

And I sat down.

Mama said, Here, drink this. She gave me something that burned like fire. I almost choked. I found out later it was whiskey! Imagine that! She thought I was going to faint.

26

I wasn't about to faint, I just thought I was out of my mind. I asked, How did Judy get here?

Then Judy began to cry. She cried hard, and kept saying, You said you were going away. I thought you'd never come home. I was bad. You said you'd leave me there. You were mad at me.

I put my arm around her and said, Judy, I might get a little mad but I'd never go away and leave you. (That's just what I did, though.)

I tried to explain. I thought you were lost. I looked all over the store for you. Why didn't you stay at the doll counter? Where did you go?

They all started to talk at once. It took a while before I could understand. What do you think happened? She thought I really had gone away and left her. So she went out on the street and started walking home. She walked a long way, till she got so tired she couldn't walk any more. Then she didn't know where she was, and started to cry, and a lady found her and brought her home, just a little while after I phoned. Thank goodness she knew her address!

Then Mama started in on me. Where were *you* all this time? Why did you hang up and leave me worrying? When the woman brought Judy home I almost went crazy. We were sitting here waiting, and I was going to call the police, but Papa said, No, wait a while longer.

Papa was standing there, not saying a word, but his face was twisted into a scowl. And Dave was looking all shook up.

Then it hit me. It was *me* they were upset about. They were worried sick because Joanne and Marcy had come in and told them where we were, and they called the store and nobody could find me. Mama said they called my name on the loudspeaker but I never heard it. I guess I was too upset to hear anything.

Mama was afraid I was going to run away. I thought she must be a mind reader.

Well, after a while we calmed down and had supper. Mama put the kids to bed, and I went in and kissed Judy goodnight. Then I went to the kitchen. Mama was washing the dishes and Papa was sitting there watching her. And Dave was drying. I guess it was the first time I ever saw him do it.

I stood there and stared at the floor. I was waiting for them to talk. I expected them to say I ought to be punished. And if they did, I knew I deserved it. But I wanted to tell them how I felt, why it happened. Only I wasn't sure how to say it, so I waited.

Then Mama said, Debbie, I know you'll never do

it again. When I thought you were lost, it took ten years off my life.

I said, I'm sorry.

She said, I know you are. But I want to tell you I'm sorry too. You should have told me before that you wanted to go shopping.

I said, I guess I should have. But I'm not all that crazy about shopping. I didn't really want to go shopping.

Mama said, Well, I don't understand you.

But Papa said, Debbie, suppose you tell us what you *do* want.

I looked at him and saw he really wanted to know. And I wanted to tell him. I wanted to say, I only want what everybody else in this family gets.

But I couldn't say a thing like that, after they were so worried about me. I tried to think of some one thing that would stand for it. And what do you think I said?

A trumpet.

All three of them stared at me as if I was talking Chinese. Then my brother Dave understood. He said, Good idea!

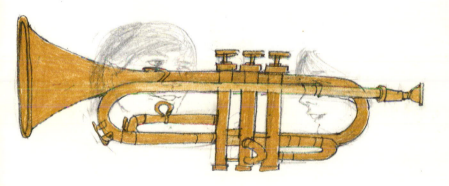

So that's what I got out of my shopping trip. That and something else. Not a thing you can see or touch, but a new way of thinking—about people, and about me. And it feels good.

ABOUT THE AUTHOR

ELEANOR CLYMER lives in a small country village, but she was born and spent most of her life in New York City. She knows at first hand the atmosphere of the crowded, busy streets, the subway trains and department stores that form the background for *How I Went Shopping and What I Got.* The idea for this story came to her when she saw a little girl being shepherded through a store by a big sister.

Mrs. Clymer has written forty-three books for children, and she is constantly adding to that list. She and her husband live in Katonah, New York.

ABOUT THE ARTIST

TRINA SCHART HYMAN began drawing professionally at the age of eighteen and has since illustrated numerous books for children. About her pictures she says, "I never use models, and rarely have to resort to reference material. I am fortunate in having a good retentive memory for the way people and things look. The basis for all my illustrations is line drawing; usually pen and ink or brush and ink, sometimes pencil or ballpoint pen. I read a manuscript through anywhere from two to a dozen times before I begin work, and refer to it constantly while working."

Miss Hyman lives in Lyme, New Hampshire.